JN074059

人生の

How To Swim Through Your Life

泳ぎ方

HONDA　Tsuyoshi

本田 つよし

How To Swim
Through Your Life

序文

　私は、仏教を勉強するにつれて、日本語より英語で学んだほう
が、その本質を理解しやすいということに気がつきました。ご
存じのとおり、仏教にはたくさんの専門用語、とくに漢字の言
葉があり、これらが学びを妨げています。ところが、英語を通
してなら、多くの場合、この問題は驚くほど簡単に解決してし
まいます。

　ここで、ケネス田中先生のことに触れないわけにはいきません。
実は、先生との出会いは幸運な偶然でした。2018 年、私は自
宅近くのブックオフで、先生の書かれた『真宗入門』という本
をたまたま見つけて購入しました。そしてこの本には『Ocean』
という英語の原書があることを知り、もちろんためらうことな
く、アマゾンで買って取り寄せたのです。そして、またしても
偶然に、仏教伝道協会で、「仏教を英語で学ぶ」クラスがあり、
それも何とケネス先生が講師であることを知ったのです！ 実
際、これらのことはすべてほとんど同時に起きました。後から
考えてみれば、阿弥陀様のお導きだったのでしょう。ケネス先
生のご指導のもと、私は仏教の本質を学び続けており、今、仏

教について英語で三冊目の詩集を出版できるまでになったのです。

私と関わりのあるすべての人びとへ心からの感謝を込めて。

本田つよし

Preface

While learning the Buddhist teachings, I found that it is easier to understand their essence through English rather than through Japanese. As you know, there are lots of technical terms, especially in Chinese character, Kanji, which prevent you from learning. But through English, this problem is solved amazingly with ease in many cases.

Here, I must not forget to mention Kenneth Tanaka Sensei. In fact, the encounter with him was a lucky co-incidence. In 2018, I happened to find his work "*Shinshu Nyūmon*" at BOOK-OFF near my house, and bought it. And I found that this book has an original version in English, "Ocean". Of course, with no hesitation, I purchased "Ocean" at AMAZON. Then again, I happened to know that there was a class "Buddhism through English" at Bukkyo Dendo Kyokai by, surprisingly, Kenneth Sensei himself! Actually, all these things happened almost at the same time. I think Amida guided me to Kenneth Sensei, with the wisdom of hindsight. Anyway, I have been learning the essence of the Buddhist teachings under the guidance of Kenneth Sensei and now I have been able to publish my THIRD anthology in English on Buddhism.

With my heartfelt gratitude to all the people related to me.

HONDA Tsuyoshi

Contents

Ocean

(In Gratitude to Kenneth Tanaka Sensei ※)

例えばあなたが海に
ひとり取り残されて
どこへ行くか全くわからず
泳ごうともがけばもがくほど
溺れてしまいそうだとしたら

そんな時は
ただ力を抜いて
もがくのを止め
今いるその場所つまり海に
すべてを委ねることだ

きっとあなたを超える何か
はかりしれない何かが
あなたを抱きしめ
支えてくれているかのように
もう溺れていないことに
気づくだろう

Suppose you are left alone
In the ocean,
Not knowing which way to go
And the more you strive to swim,
The more likely you will drown.

At such time
Just let go,
Let go of your striving
And leave everything to the ocean
Where you are now.

You will surely become aware
That you're not drowning any more
As if something beyond you,
Something immeasurable is
Embracing you,
Supporting you.

力を抜いて
もがくのを止め
大いなる存在に気づいて
すべてを委ねよう

それこそが
人生を泳ぎ切る方法なのだ

※「真宗入門：ケネス・タナカ」法蔵館 p2-3
Kenneth K. Tanaka. *Ocean*. WisdomOcean Publications, pp. 1-3.

Let go,

Let go of your striving,

Awaken to Something Great

And leave everything to it.

That's just how

You swim through life.

Flower

花は
時が来れば咲き
時が来れば
散っていく

すべてのいのちは
しかるべき時に
現れては消える

何という奇跡！
すべての後ろには
大いなる存在が
控えているに違いない

A flower blossoms
In due time.
A flower is out of bloom
In due time.

Every life
Comes and goes
In due time.

What a miracle!
There must be
Something Great
Behind everything.

Everything Is Changing

すべては変化している
つまり
どんなことでも
悪い方へと変化しうる

でもそれは
どんなことでも
あなたが良い方向に変えられる
という意味でもあるのだ

できないことを
できることに
変えられる人生は
何て
素晴らしいのだろう！

Everything is changing.
That means
Anything can change
For the worse.

But it also means
You could change
Anything
For the better.

You could change
What you cannot do
Into what you can do.
How wonderful
Your life is!

Jewel

自分の外側に
宝石を探しても
見つからない

自分の内側に
宝石を探しても
充分ではない

あなたは宝石を
所有しているのではなく
あなたが宝石そのものだ
ということに気づきなさい

Searching for a jewel

Outside you

Is not achievable.

Searching for a jewel

Inside you

Is not sufficient.

Just come to realize that

It's not that you HAVE a jewel,

But you ARE

A jewel itself.

Mindful Life

マインドフルに生きるとは
丁寧に生きるということ

歩く時、食べる時
家事をする時
ひとつひとつの動作を
丁寧に行えば
生活の質が
違ってくる

マインドフルな仕事とは
心の行き届いた仕事
四角い部屋を
丸く掃くのではなく
隅々にまで
心を行き届かせれば
その仕事が
あなたという人を表す
証_{あかし}になる

To live mindfully is

To live with care.

When you walk, eat,

And do housework,

Every action

Done with care

Will make quality of your life

Different.

A mindful job is

An attentive job.

Not sweeping a square room

In a circle,

But doing attentive job

To every corner

Will lead to the evidence

To show

What you are.

Falling

人は時々ころぶ
前に進み続けるかぎり
人は
時々ころぶ

でも
ころぶことは
決して失敗ではない

ころぶことを恐れて
前に進むのを
止めた時
ころぶことは
本当の
失敗になる

You sometimes fall.
As long as you keep
Moving forward,
You sometimes fall.

However,
Falling is
Never a failure.

When you stop
Moving forward
By being afraid of
Falling,
It will become
A true failure.

The Path

物事は
起こるように起こる
単純なことだ
種も仕掛けも無い

だから自分で創り出した
ややこしい迷路で
迷うのは止めよう

ただ
目の前の道を
歩いていこう

物事は
起こるように起こる
すべてを受け入れて
前に進み続ければ
それでいいのだ

Things happen
As they happen.
It's simple,
No tricks or gimmicks.

So don't get lost
In the complicated maze
You have created yourself.

Just step forward
On the path
In front of you.

Things happen
As they happen.
It's OK for you
To accept everything
And keep moving forward.

Nobody But You

恵まれない環境に生まれ
人一倍大変だけれど
幸せな人生というのは
きっとある

恵まれた環境に生まれ
みんなに羨ましがられても
不幸な人生というのは
きっとある

何より大切なのは
心の置きどころと
どう行動するか

幸せかそうでないかは
他の誰でもなく
あなた次第なのだ

Born in an unlucky environment,
Struggling more than others,
Yet happy life
There must be.

Born in a lucky environment,
Envied by everybody
Yet unhappy life
There must be.

What matters most is
Where you put your mind
And how you act.

Whether you are happy or not
Depends on
Nobody but you.

Practice With Faith

信仰は時に
あなたを裏切るが
実践は常に
成果をもたらす

実践なき信仰は
危険でさえあり
あなたを間違った場所へ
連れてゆきかねない

瞑想にせよ
念仏にせよ
信仰とともに実践しよう

必ずあなたは
しかるべき場所に
たどり着くだろう

While faith sometimes
Betrays you,
Practice always
Pays off.

Faith without practice
Could be even dangerous.
It might lead you
To the wrong place.

Be it meditation,
Oral recitation,
Practice with faith.

It would definitely
Lead you
To where you should be.

Deeper, Higher, Closer

この世界の
横の軸を
ただ彷徨うだけの時
人生に
縦の軸を持とう

自分の内側を
深く掘り下げれば下げるほど
より高いところに
大いなる存在のより近くに
手が届くから

人生に
縦の軸を持とう

When you're just wandering aimlessly
On the horizontal axis
Of this world,
Have your vertical axis
In life.

The deeper you
Dig down within yourself,
The higher you will be able to
Reach for,
The closer to Something Great.

Have a vertical axis
In your life.

Chain Reaction Of Happiness

あなたが幸せになりたいなら
あなたのまわりの人たちも
幸せであるべきだ

ブッダが言うように
幸せは分け合っても
決して減ることはない

もっと言えば
あなたの幸せが
他人の幸せを生み
他人の幸せこそが
きっとあなたの幸せを
生むものなのだ

If you want to be happy,
People around you
Should also be happy.

As the Buddha says,
Happiness never decreases
By being shared.

Furthermore,
Your happiness produces
Others' happiness.
And it is others' happiness
That surely produces
Your happiness.

Others

他者を
敵と見なすことが
つねに戦争へとつながっていく

他者を
友と見なすことが
やがて平和をもたらす

他者への
思いやりと愛
それこそが
ブッダとイエスが
強調したこと
そしてこの世界に
最も必要なこと

To regard others

As enemy

Always leads to war.

To regard others

As friend

Eventually leads to peace.

Care and love

For others.

Those are

Just what the Buddha and Jesus

Put emphasis on,

And most necessary

For this world.

Your Life, Your Light

AIを
あなたの光にしない
アルゴリズムを
あなたの光にしない

ブッダの言葉にあるように
あなた自身を
あなたの光にしなさい

そうでないと
あなたの人生は
誰か他の人のものになる

あなたの人生を
本当にあなたのものにしなさい

Do not make AI
The light for you.
Do not make algorithm
The light for you.

Just make yourself
The light for you,
As the Buddha said.

Otherwise,
Your life would become
Someone else's life.

Just make your life
Truly yours.

Give And Given

誰かにしてあげたことは
さっさと忘れ
自分にしてもらったことは
心に留める

それが
迷いなく
しっかりとした人生を
送る道

Just forget

What you give to someone.

Do remember

What is given to you.

That's the way

You keep your life

Stable

With no waver.

Truth

真実は
普通のものにある
真実は
あなたの日常生活にある
真実は
あなたの中にある

だから
何か途方もないものを探したり
無理に日常生活を
特別なものにしたり
あなた以外の
誰かになろうと
する必要はありません

The truth is
In something ordinary.
The truth is
In your daily life.
The truth is
In you.

So, you need not seek
Something extraordinary,
Need not forcibly make
Your daily life special,
Need not become
Someone other than
You.

Compassionate Words

ネガティブな発言に気をつけて
ネガティブな言葉で話すことは
一種の暴力で
自分にとっては毒を飲むこと

ネガティブな発言に気をつけて
それは人間関係を壊し
あなた自身のやる気をそぐ

ネガティブな発言に気をつけて
それよりいつも
思いやりのある愛語を
口にしよう

Beware of negative speech.
Talking with a negative word is
A kind of violence and
Taking poison for yourself.

Beware of negative speech.
It deteriorates relationship and
Discourages yourself.

Beware of negative speech.
Rather,
Speak compassionate words
All the time.

Beware Of The Negative

ネガティブは
炎のように
その熱で
人を惹きつける

でも
気をつけて
ネガティブに近づきすぎると
必ず
火傷するから

ネガティブとは距離を保とう
それは心を焼け焦げにし
取り返しのつかない
ダメージを残すから

The negative is
Something like a flame
That attracts you
With its heat.

However,
Beware of the negative.
That will surely burn you
When you come
Too close to it.

Keep away from the negative.
Because it will scorch your heart
And will leave you
Fatally damaged.

No Attachment

あなたを傷つけたり
脅したりする言葉に
反応するのではなく
ただ
聞き流してしまいなさい

あなたを迷わせる思いに
とらわれるのではなく
ただ
手放してしまいなさい

あなたがあなたでいるために
最も大切なのは
執着を持たないことなのです

Do not react to

The word that hurts or

Threatens you,

But just listen to it

With no attention.

Do not get attached to

The thought that confuses you,

But just

Let it go.

To be as you are,

What matters most is

To have no attachment.

Supreme Happiness

何ものにも
とらわれず
心は平和

これ以上の
幸せが
あるだろうか？

Having

No attachment

But peace of mind.

Is there

Any greater happiness

Than this?

No Multitasking

いっぺんに
多くのことを片付けようと
焦ってはならない

一度に一つのことを
心をこめて成し遂げ
それから
次のことに取り掛かる

それが
人生が上手く進み
何よりも
心穏やかでいられる方法だ

Do not rush

To get many things done

At one time.

Get one thing done

At a time

With wholeheartedness

And then get another done.

That's the way

To be successful

And to be peaceful above all

In your life.

Clear Water

あちこち違う場所を
次から次へと
掘るのは止めにしよう

手に入るのは
泥水だ

一つの場所に
集中し
心を込めて
掘り続ければ

間違いなく
きれいな水が手に入る

Stop trying to dig holes

One after another

In the different spots.

All you can get is

Muddy water.

Just try focusing

On one spot

And dig there

Single-mindedly.

You will definitely get

Clear water.

Seeking The Path

道を求め続ける限り
あなたは
前進し続けている

時には
同じところで
ひっかかってしまい
ちっとも前に進まないと
感じるかもしれない

でも真実は違う
道を求め続ける限り
あなたは
前進し続けている

心が道を求めるのを
止めた時
あなたの進歩も止まるのだ

As long as you keep
Seeking the path
You are moving forward.

Sometimes
You might feel
Not moving forward
As if being stuck
At the same place.

But it's not true.
As long as you keep
Seeking the path
You are moving forward.

When your mind stops
Seeking the path,
Your progress stops.

True Answer

本やネットで
見つけた答えは
まだ
あなたの
本当の答えではない

自分の五感で体験し
自分の行動で
確かめてみて
初めて
それは
あなたの
本当の答えになる

An answer

That you have found

In a book or on the Internet

Is not yet

Your true answer.

Only after experienced

Through your five senses

And convinced

Through your action,

It will become

Your true answer

For the first time.

Compassion And Wisdom

智慧なき慈悲は
独りよがりで
危険なものにさえなりかねない

他者を助けるどころか
傷つけるかもしれない
そして時には
諸刃の剣のように
あなた自身を傷つけるかもしれない

慈悲なき智慧は
独りよがりで
危険なものにさえなりかねない

それは行き過ぎると
反感を招き
あなたを世界から
孤立させるかもしれない

慈悲と智慧は

Compassion without wisdom
Might become complacent
And even dangerous.

It could do harm to others
Rather than helping them,
And sometimes
Do harm to yourself
Like a double-edged sword.

Wisdom without compassion
Might become complacent
And even dangerous.

It could provoke antipathy
When it goes too far,
And could isolate you
From the world.

Compassion and wisdom

鳥が高く飛ぶための

二枚の羽のように

互いに補うべきものなのだ

Should complement each other

Like two wings of a bird

To fly high.

The Essence Of The Universe

いのちとは
あなたが両親から
受け継いだもの

そして両親は
いのちを
先祖から受け継ぎ

先祖は
動物から
魚から
微生物から
いのちを受け継いだ

そしてそれらの存在はすべて
いのちを
宇宙から受け継いだ

つまりあなたは
宇宙の精髄（エッセンス）を受け継いだ

Life is something
You have taken over
From your parents.

And your parents
Took it over
From your ancestors.

Your ancestors
Had taken it over
From animals,
From fish,
And from microbes.

And all those beings
Took over life
From the universe.

So you are the being
That has taken over

存在なのだ

The essence of the universe.

Immeasurable

真の意味で
人間を計ることはできない
世界を計ることはできない
宇宙を計ることはできない

すべてを計ることができると
信じた時
人は滅びるだろう

今日の計りは
明日には役に立たなくなる
かもしれない

そしてまさに
人間の計りを超えた存在が
アミダ
そのもともとの名前は
「計り知れない光」なのだ

In the true sense,

You cannot measure humanity.

You cannot measure the world.

You cannot measure the universe.

When people believe that

Everything is measurable,

They will probably perish.

A today's measure

Might not be able to work

Tomorrow.

And the very presence

That transcends man's measure is

Amida

Whose original name is

"Immeasurable light."

ONE

あなたが
この宇宙に
存在している
という事実そのことが
あなたは宇宙と
一体であり
偉大な存在と
一体である
という真実を表している

だから悩むことはない
気づいていても
気づいていなくても
あなたはすでに
救われています

The fact itself that you are here

In the universe

Represents the truth

That you are

ONE

With the universe,

That you are

ONE

With Something Great.

So, don't worry.

You have already been

Saved

Whether you may

Notice it or not.

Nembutsu

念仏を唱える時は
真心をこめなさい

言い換えれば
あなたの中に
何も残らなくなるまで
自分を解き放つのです

するとアミダが必ず
あなたの真空に流れ込み
あなたとアミダは
ひとつになります

念仏とは
そういうものなのです

When you recite nembutsu,
Do it wholeheartedly.

In other words,
Let yourself go
Until nothing is left
Within you.

Then Amida will surely flow into
Your vacuum,
And you and Amida
Will become ONE.

That's
What nembutsu is.

I Feel Amida

起きて
アミダを感じ
寝て
アミダを感じる

心定まるとき
アミダを感じ
心乱れるとき
アミダを感じる

幸せなとき
アミダを感じ
幸せでないとき
アミダを感じる

アミダとは
私にとって
大いなる存在の別名

何とありがたい

When I wake up,
I feel Amida.
When I fall asleep,
I feel Amida.

When I am determined,
I feel Amida.
When I am confused,
I feel Amida.

When I am happy,
I feel Amida.
When I am unhappy,
I feel Amida.

Amida is
Another name for Something Great
For me.

I am so grateful

そんなアミダと私は
ひとつなのだ

That such Amida and I are
ONE.

Only Gratitude

アミダに
助けを求めない
いつも
助けてくれている

アミダに
救いを求めない
すでに
救ってくれている

やるべきは
求めることではなく
感謝の心を持って
念仏を唱えることだ

I do not ask Amida
To help me,
Because he is always
Helping me.

I do not ask Amida
To save me,
Because he has already
Saved me.

All I have to do is
Not to ask,
But to recite nembutsu
With feelings of gratitude.

Every Morning

毎朝
私は目を覚ます

毎朝
私は生きている

何という奇跡！
寝ているあいだに
死ななかったのだ

毎朝
私は生きている

毎朝
私は感謝する

生きることは
すべてが奇跡だということに
気がつくことだ

Every morning
I wake up.

Every morning
I am alive.

What a miracle!
I have not died
While I was sleeping.

Every morning
I am alive.

Every morning
I am grateful.

To live is
To be aware that
Everything is a miracle.

Sacred Torch Of Life

早い朝
新聞配達の音が聞こえる

そこで私は思う
いったい何人の人びとが
私がこの世界で生きていくために
働いてくれているのだろうと

早い朝
太陽が昇るのを見る

そこで私は思う
いったい何人の人びとが
この宇宙に私が存在するために
いのちの聖火を
リレーしてくれたのだろう

願わくば私の聖火が燃え盛り
他者を明るく照らして
幸せにしてくれますように

Early in the morning
I hear a newsboy delivering.

Now I am wondering
How many people there are
Working for me to live
In this world.

Early in the morning
I watch the sun rising.

Now I am wondering
How many people there have been
Relaying the sacred torch of life
That made me come into being
In this universe.

I wish for my sacred torch burn fully
Illuminating others
And making them happy.

Be A Bodhisattva For Someone

人は誰も
慈悲と感謝を心に備えて
生まれてくる

その慈悲と感謝を
損なわずにいたら
困った時には必ず
誰かが助けの菩薩となって
あなたの元に現れる

なぜならば慈悲と感謝は
もう一組の慈悲と感謝を
引き寄せるからだ

ということは
次に誰かが困っている時
その人の菩薩になるのは
きっとあなただ

Everyone is born

With compassion and gratitude

In his or her heart.

If you keep your compassion and gratitude

Intact,

Someone will surely come up to you

As a bodhisattva to help you,

When you're in trouble.

Because compassion and gratitude

Attract another pair of

Compassion and gratitude.

That means

You can surely be a bodhisattva

For someone in trouble

Next time.

HONDA Tsuyoshi

本田つよし

Profile

プロフィール

Born in Kumamoto Prefecture. Graduated from Waseda University.

熊本県生まれ。早稲田大学第一文学部英文学科卒業。

Weblog "English for Happiness"　ブログ「しあわせになる英語」

https://www.englishforhappiness.com/

Twitter　ツイッター

https://twitter.com/englishforhapp

A member of the Steering Committee of "Sangha for Studying and Practicing Buddhism Through Basic English"

「仏教を初歩英語で学び実践するサンガの会」運営委員

人生の泳ぎ方
How To Swim Through Your Life

発行日　　2022 年 10 月 10 日　第 1 刷発行

著者　　　本田 つよし（ほんだ・つよし）

発行者　　田辺修三
発行所　　東洋出版株式会社
　　　　　〒 112-0014　東京都文京区関口 1-23-6
　　　　　電話　03-5261-1004（代）　振替　00110-2-175030
　　　　　http://www.toyo-shuppan.com/

印刷・製本　日本ハイコム株式会社